A MAGIC CHARM™ BOOK BY ELIZABETH KODA-CALLAN

The

MAGIC LOCKET

Story and Pictures
by
Elizabeth Koda-Callan

WORKMAN PUBLISHING, NEW YORK

Library of Congress Cataloging-in-Publication Data is available.

ISBN 0-7611-3636-3

Workman books are available at special discounts when purchased in bulk for
premiums and sales promotions as well as for fund-raising or educational use.
Special editions or book excerpts can also be created to specification.
For details, contact the Special Sales Director at the address below.

Workman Publishing Company, Inc.
708 Broadway
New York, New York 10003-9555

www.workman.com

Printed in China

First Printing October 2004

10 9 8 7 6 5 4 3 2 1

For Jennifer
with Love

Once there was a little girl who couldn't do anything right. Not that she didn't try!

In the morning, when she brushed her teeth, the toothpaste wouldn't stay on the brush.

When she dressed herself, the front was always in the back and the back was always in the front.

She tried to do her math at school, but somehow two plus two never made four.

She tried to feed her dolls, but the cat got fed instead.

She helped with the groceries, but some things couldn't be helped.

Day after day went by, and the little girl got very discouraged.

One afternoon, after school, the little girl was rushing home. She raced across the yard and through the back door of her house. It was then that she bumped into the table in the kitchen.

"Ouch!" she cried.

"Oh, dear," said a voice.

The little girl looked up. There in the kitchen was her Great Aunt Emma.

"Well, hello," said her great aunt. "It's wonderful to see you again. You're just in time for tea."

Great Aunt Emma had a sweet face and kindly eyes, and her hair was red just like the little girl's. She was the little girl's favorite.

9

Aunt Emma smiled. "You know," she said, "I was very much like you when I was a girl. The way you rushed in here just reminded me. I was always upsetting the apple cart."

When the little girl's mother went into the pantry to get some tea cakes, Aunt Emma picked up the steaming teapot and poured tea for them all. The little girl noticed how carefully her aunt held the pot and poured each cup full. She never spilled a drop. Aunt Emma may have made a mess of things as a girl, but she certainly wasn't that way anymore.

Aunt Emma reached into her purse. "I have a gift for you," she said. She pulled out a ball of pink tissue paper that was tied with a beautiful satin bow. The little girl unwrapped the package and there, within the folds of the tissue paper, was a shiny golden locket.

"This was given to me by my mother," said Aunt Emma, "and now I would like you to have it. It is a magical locket. If you wear it, it can help you do whatever you want. That is, if you believe in it."

The little girl, being the kind of little girl she was, didn't completely believe her aunt. But she smiled, took the locket, and thanked her.

After tea with the little girl and her mother, it was time for Aunt Emma to leave.

"Thank you for a lovely visit, my dear." she said.

The little girl walked her great aunt to the door, gave her a big hug, and watched her disappear down the street.

The little girl looked at the locket. It was a beautiful, shiny golden color that glinted in the sun, but she really didn't believe it was magical.

That day she did her favorite things. She jumped rope. She played on the swings. She played ball. Even though she was busy, she kept thinking about the locket.

It had a hinge on one side. She tried to open it, but the locket was closed shut.

That evening, she took the locket to her room and put it on the table by her bed.

The next morning, when she woke up, the little girl stretched and went to the closet to get her clothes. Then she remembered the locket. She remembered what her great aunt had said. Could it really be magical? She walked back and put the locket on. The little girl held the locket tightly for a moment, and found herself saying, "I believe in you." Then, very slowly and carefully, she dressed herself.

The following morning, as soon as she woke up, the little girl put on the locket again, held it tightly, and said, "I believe in you." She held it again the next morning, and the next, and the next.

And here's what happened.

When she brushed her teeth, the toothpaste stayed right on the brush.

When she dressed herself, the front
was in front and the back was in back.

When she did her math, two plus two equaled four.

When she fed her dolls, everyone enjoyed the party except the cat.

When she helped with the groceries,
even the eggs were safe.

The little girl was overjoyed. She really could do everything she wanted to do!

Soon she began to wonder what made the locket so powerful. It wasn't long before she found out.

One morning, when she was putting on the locket, it slipped through her fingers and fell to the floor. When the locket fell, it snapped open. The little girl bent down to pick it up and was very surprised to see what was inside.

Inside the locket was a mirror, and in the mirror was her very own reflection.

"Why, it's me!" she thought. "It's really me. *I'm* the magic in the locket."

From then on, the little girl wore the locket every day. Every day she held the locket tightly and whispered, "I believe in you." The locket was filled with her own special magic and from that day on she was never without it.

About the Author

Elizabeth Koda-Callan is a designer, illustrator, and bestselling children's book author who lives in New York City. Her own childhood memories about the awkward part of growing up have inspired this story.

She is the creator of the Magic Charm Books™ series, which includes THE SILVER SLIPPERS, THE GOOD LUCK PONY, THE TINY ANGEL, THE SHINY SKATES, THE CAT NEXT DOOR, THE TWO BEST FRIENDS, THE QUEEN OF HEARTS, THE STORYTELLER, THE SECRET DIARY, and THE ARTIST'S PALETTE, as well as the interactive children's book, THE SQUIGGLY WIGGLYS.